WALT DISNEY'S
Favorite Nursery Tales

The Gingerbread Man
and
The Golden Goose

A GOLDEN BOOK • NEW YORK

Western Publishing Company, Inc.

Racine, Wisconsin 53404

The Gingerbread Man

One day Daisy Duck was very busy in her kitchen. It was Donald Duck's birthday, and she was baking him a special treat. She was baking him a gingerbread man. He had currants for eyes and a cherry for a nose and three currant buttons down his front.

When the gingerbread man was done, Daisy put him on the windowsill to cool while she went out into the garden to pick some daisies.

As soon as she had gone, the Gingerbread Man
jumped off the windowsill and ran down the path.
Daisy saw him, and she called, "Stop! Stop!"

And Donald saw him and called, "Stop! Stop!"
But the Gingerbread Man laughed and shouted, "Run, run, as fast as you can. You can't catch me; I'm the Gingerbread Man!"

Out of the gate and into the field they all ran, and there was Goofy, resting under a tree.

"Stop! Stop!" he called when he saw the Gingerbread Man and Daisy and Donald. But still the Gingerbread Man didn't stop.

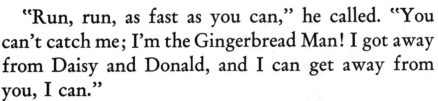

"Run, run, as fast as you can," he called. "You can't catch me; I'm the Gingerbread Man! I got away from Daisy and Donald, and I can get away from you, I can."

And on he ran, with Daisy and Donald and Goofy close behind.

Soon they came to the part of the country-side where Mickey was tending a gaggle of geese. The Gingerbread Man saw the geese crossing on the road ahead, but he *still* didn't slow down. He kept right on running, scattering the geese as he passed by. Mickey yelled to him, "Stop! Stop!" But the Gingerbread Man only laughed and shouted, "Run, run, as fast as you can. You can't catch me; I'm the Gingerbread Man. I got away from Daisy and Donald and Goofy, and I can get away from you, I can." So Mickey, feeling hungry, joined in the chase, too.

Around the barn they ran, and there were Chip
and Dale, swinging on a straw swing. "Time for tea,"
they said when they saw the special Gingerbread
Man, and they called, "Stop! Stop!"

But the Gingerbread Man laughed and shouted,
"Run, run, as fast as you can. You can't catch me;
I'm the Gingerbread Man! I got away from Daisy
and Donald and Goofy and Mickey Mouse, and I can
get away from you, I can." And he ran faster than
ever, with the others close behind.

Soon the Gingerbread Man came to a stream, and there was the Big Bad Wolf, dabbling his toes in the water. The wolf saw the Gingerbread Man, and he saw Chip and Dale and Mickey and Goofy and Donald and Daisy chasing after him.

"Jump on my back, Gingerbread Man, and I'll take you across the stream, away from all those greedy people," the wolf said.

So the Gingerbread Man jumped on his back, and
the Big Bad Wolf started swimming.

"Wolf, I am getting wet," said the Gingerbread
Man presently.

"Then jump on my head," said the wolf.

"Wolf, I am getting wet even here."

"Then jump on my nose," said the wolf.

So the Gingerbread Man jumped on the wolf's nose,
and, gobble and crunch, the Big Bad Wolf had eaten
him up in a minute—which, after all, is what gingerbread men are made for in the first place!

The Golden Goose

Once upon a time, a woodcutter had a son who was considered foolish by some. He was nicknamed Goofy. But, as you shall see, Goofy became happier and richer than the woodcutter and all his other sons put together, for Goofy had a kind heart.

Out in the woods one day, Goofy met a little old man. "Will you share your lunch with me?" asked the little old man.

"Why, ah, sure—happy to," said Goofy.

"You are kinder than your brothers," said the little old man. "When I asked them, they refused to share. Look under that bush. You will find your reward."

Under the bush, Goofy found a goose that had feathers of purest gold. Goofy took hold of the goose's leash and set off to see the world.

Soon he came to an inn and sat down to a meal. Now, the innkeeper was Scrooge McDuck, and Scrooge took an instant fancy to the golden goose. When Goofy's back was turned, Scrooge touched the goose—and his hand stuck to her! He couldn't get away! Angrily, he called Huey, Dewey, and Louie.

Huey tried to pull Scrooge away, but he stuck to Scrooge. Dewey tried to pull Huey away, but *he* stuck to *Huey*. And then *Louie* stuck to *Dewey*.

Along came Minnie Mouse, in her best straw bonnet. She laughed when she saw the four of them stuck together that way.

"Ooh, a new game!" she cried and took hold of Louie, and then *she* was stuck. So Goofy had to take them all along with him. They did look silly.

When they came to the village, they met Ludwig
von Drake. "This is a preposterous, ridiculous sight,"
he snorted. "Why are you stuck together? I know
how to solve this silly situation." (Ludwig von Drake
always spoke that way.)

But no sooner had he laid hold of Minnie than he,
too, was stuck. Ludwig was very cross indeed, but
yell as he might, it did no good. He was still stuck.

So Goofy went on his way, followed by Scrooge McDuck and Huey and Dewey and Louie and Minnie Mouse and Ludwig von Drake.

Now, it so happened that the road led past a castle where lived a sad princess who didn't know how to smile. Her father, the king, had tried everything to make her smile, but the poor little princess grew more and more sad.

That day, when the princess looked out of her window, she saw a strange sight.

There was Goofy marching along with the golden goose— and behind them came Scrooge McDuck and Huey and Dewey and Louie and Minnie Mouse and Ludwig von Drake (still muttering angrily in scientific language).

The princess stared in amazement. Then a most peculiar thing happened to her mouth—it turned up at the corners. Her eyes began to twinkle, and soon she was laughing so hard she could hardly stop.

When the delighted king saw what had happened, he invited Goofy and all the others into the palace for tea and cakes, and he told Goofy he could have any reward he wanted.

Grinning shyly, Goofy said that, first of all, he would like to have all his friends unstuck from the golden goose and each other. (Since kings can do anything, that was very easy.)

Then, Goofy said, he would like to be invited to the palace every Sunday for tea, to be sure that the little princess could still smile.

And that is how Goofy, with his golden goose, became very rich and happy, even though he was considered foolish by some.